First French

AT HOME

Kathy Gemmell and Jenny Tyler
Illustrated by Sue Stitt
Designed by Diane Thistlethwaite

Consultants: Sarah-Lou Reekie and Kate Griffin

CONTENTS

First published in 1993 by Usborne Publishing Ltd.
Usborne House, 83-85 Saffron Hill
London EC1N 8RT, England.
Copyright © 1993 Usborne Publishing Ltd.
First published in America August 1993.
Printed in Portugal.
Universal Edition.

Speaking French

This book is about the Noisette family. They are going to help you learn to speak French.

Word lists

You will find a word list on every double page to tell you what the French words mean.

Bonjour
bonjoor

The little letters are to help you say the French words. Read them as if they were English words.

Je...
je

Bonne nuit
bon nwee

Non
naw

Oui
we

Salut
salew

Word list

bonjour	hello
bonjoor	
salut	hi
salew	
non	no
naw	
oui	yes
we	
je	I
je	
bonne nuit	good night
bon nwee	
à toi	your turn
ah twa	

The best way to find out how to say French words is to listen to a French person speaking. Some sounds are a bit different from English. Here are some clues to help you.

When you see a "j" in French, say it like the middle sound in "treasure". Try saying *je*, which means "I".

When you see an "n" in French, be careful. Single "n"s are usually not pronounced. Only double "n"s or "n"s which come before a,e,i,o or u are pronounced.

To say the "u" in *salut*, round your lips to say "oo" then say "ee" instead.

Say the French "r" by making a rolling sound in the back of your mouth, a bit like gargling.

Try saying out loud what each person on this page is saying.

See if you can find Delphine the mouse on each double page.

Games with word lists

You can play games with the word lists if you like. Here are some ideas.

1. Cover all the French words and see if you can say the French for each English word. Score a point for each one you can remember.

2. Time yourself and see if you can say the whole list more quickly next time.

3. Race a friend. The first one to say the French for each word scores a point. The winner is the one to score the most points.

4. Play all these games the other way around, saying the English for each French word.

À toi
Look for the *à toi* boxes in this book. There is something for you to do in each of them. À *toi* means "your turn".

Look out for the joke bubbles on some of the pages.

3

The Noisettes

Here the Noisette family are introducing themselves. *Je m'appelle* [je mapell] means "I am called" or "my name is".

Loulou has chased Delphine through the Noisette's garden. See if you can follow her route from Oncle Paul to where she is now. Which members of the family did she pass on the way?

Word list

je m'appelle je mapell	I am called
Monsieur miss yer	Mr.
Madame ma dam	Mrs.
la grand-mère la gronmair	grandma
l'oncle lonkl	uncle
la tante la tont	aunt
au revoir orvwar	goodbye

Names

Noisette nwa zet	Mirabelle meer a bel
Roger rojay	Paul pol
Sophie sofee	Hercule air kewl
Henri onree	Loulou looloo
Francine fronseen	Delphine delfeen
Jean jon	Legs legs
Robert robair	Suzanne sewz an

Je m'appelle Sophie.

Je m'appelle Roger.

Je m'appelle Hercule.

Je m'appelle Jean.

Je m'appelle Grand-mère Noisette.

Je m'appelle Francine.

Je m'appelle Henri.

Hello

Bonjour [bonjoor] means "hello". Sophie is so sleepy, she has mixed up everyone's names. Say *bonjour* for her, adding the correct name each time.

Bonjour Henri

Bonjour Grand-mère

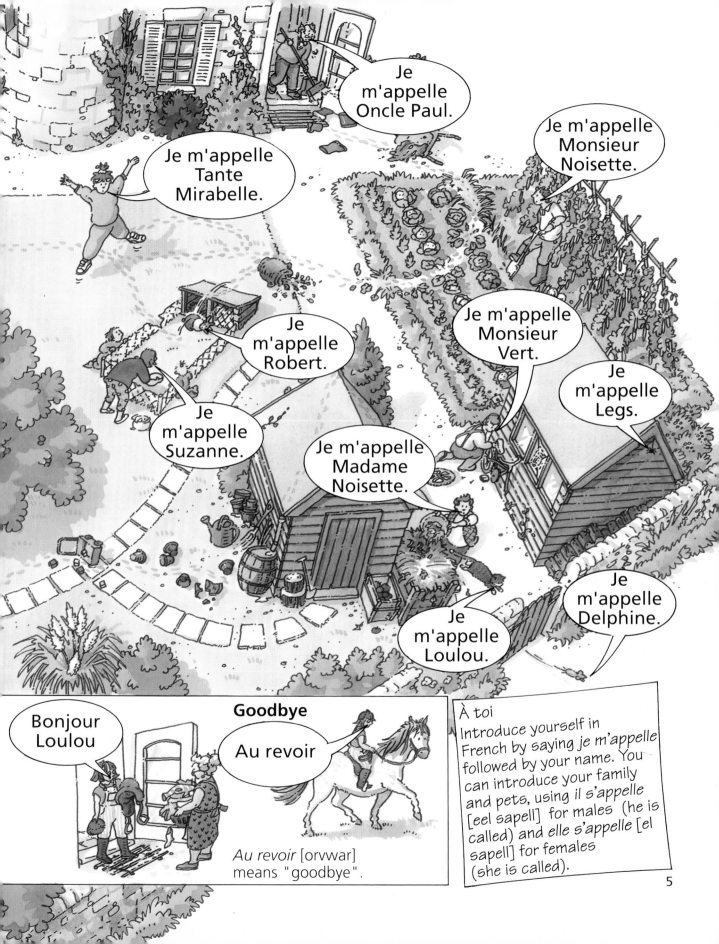

At home

Here is the inside of the Noisette family house. Can you find a way around the house, passing all those who are waiting to tell you the names of the rooms on the way? You must not pass anyone more than once.

Start at the door nearest Madame Noisette and go out by the kitchen door. (Remember that doors are not the only way to get from room to room.)

Chez nous [shay noo] means "our home". "My home" is *chez moi* [shay mwa]. Anyone else's home is *chez* then the name of the person, so "Sophie's home" would be *chez Sophie* [shay sofee].

Word list

voici	here is
vwasee	
la chambre	bedroom
la shombr	
la salle de bain	bathroom
la sal dba	
le grenier	attic
le grin ee ay	
la cave	cellar
la kaav	
la cuisine	kitchen
la kweezeen	
le salon	lounge
le salaw	
la salle à manger	dining room
la sala monjay	
la maison	house
la mayzaw	
le jardin	garden
le jarda	
maman	mum
ma maw	
chez nous	our home
shay noo	

Voici la chambre.

Voici le salon.

Voici le jardin.

Voici Maman.

Voici la maison.

7

Draw a map

Sophie and Henri have drawn a map of the area near their house and have written all the names in French.

Draw a map of your own area or somewhere you think you would like to live and label it in French.

l'église

le pont

la rivière

la ferme

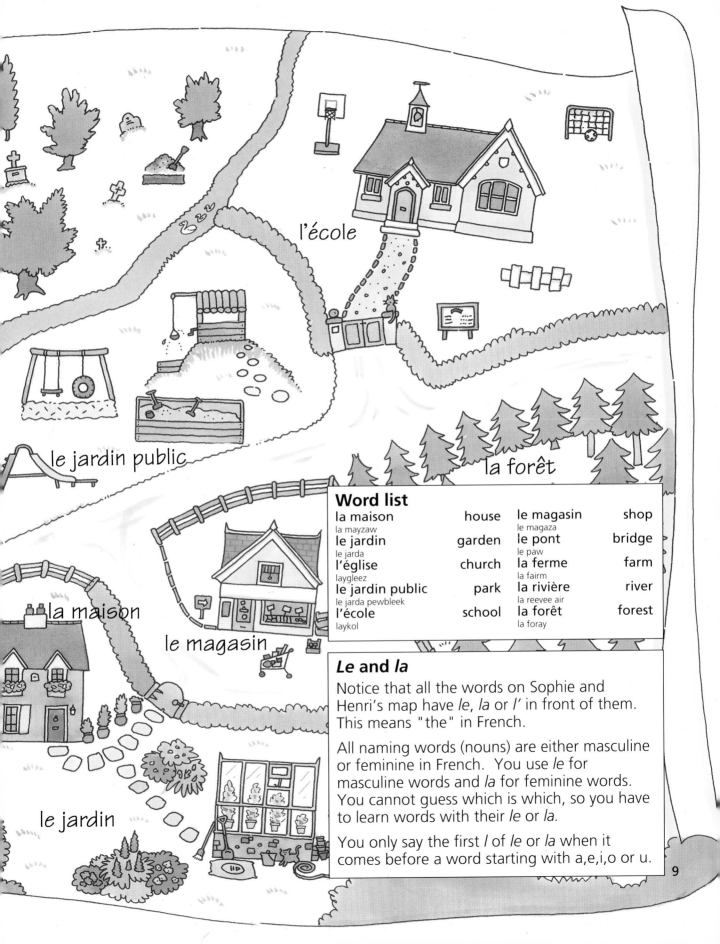

l'école

le jardin public

la forêt

la maison

le magasin

le jardin

Word list

la maison *la mayzaw*	house	le magasin *le magaza*	shop
le jardin *le jarda*	garden	le pont *le paw*	bridge
l'église *laygleez*	church	la ferme *la fairm*	farm
le jardin public *le jarda pewbleek*	park	la rivière *la reevee air*	river
l'école *laykol*	school	la forêt *la foray*	forest

Le and *la*

Notice that all the words on Sophie and Henri's map have *le*, *la* or *l'* in front of them. This means "the" in French.

All naming words (nouns) are either masculine or feminine in French. You use *le* for masculine words and *la* for feminine words. You cannot guess which is which, so you have to learn words with their *le* or *la*.

You only say the first *l* of *le* or *la* when it comes before a word starting with a,e,i,o or u.

9

Counting in French

Sophie and Henri stayed up late to finish their map and now can't sleep. In fact, everybody is counting things to help them get to sleep.

Count out loud in French for each person. Who do you think fell asleep first? Use the number list to help you.

Number list

un a	one
deux deuh	two
trois trwa	three
quatre katr	four
cinq sank	five
six seess	six
sept set	seven
huit weet	eight
neuf neuf	nine
dix deess	ten

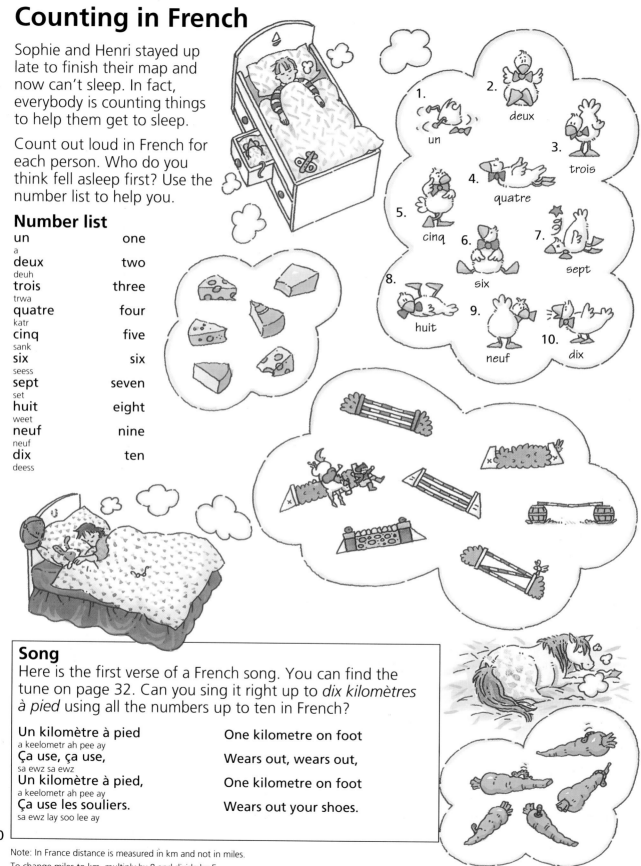

1. un
2. deux
3. trois
4. quatre
5. cinq
6. six
7. sept
8. huit
9. neuf
10. dix

Song

Here is the first verse of a French song. You can find the tune on page 32. Can you sing it right up to *dix kilomètres à pied* using all the numbers up to ten in French?

Un kilomètre à pied
a keelometr ah pee ay
Ça use, ça use,
sa ewz sa ewz
Un kilomètre à pied,
a keelometr ah pee ay
Ça use les souliers.
sa ewz lay soo lee ay

One kilometre on foot

Wears out, wears out,

One kilometre on foot

Wears out your shoes.

10

Note: In France distance is measured in km and not in miles.
To change miles to km, multiply by 8 and divide by 5.

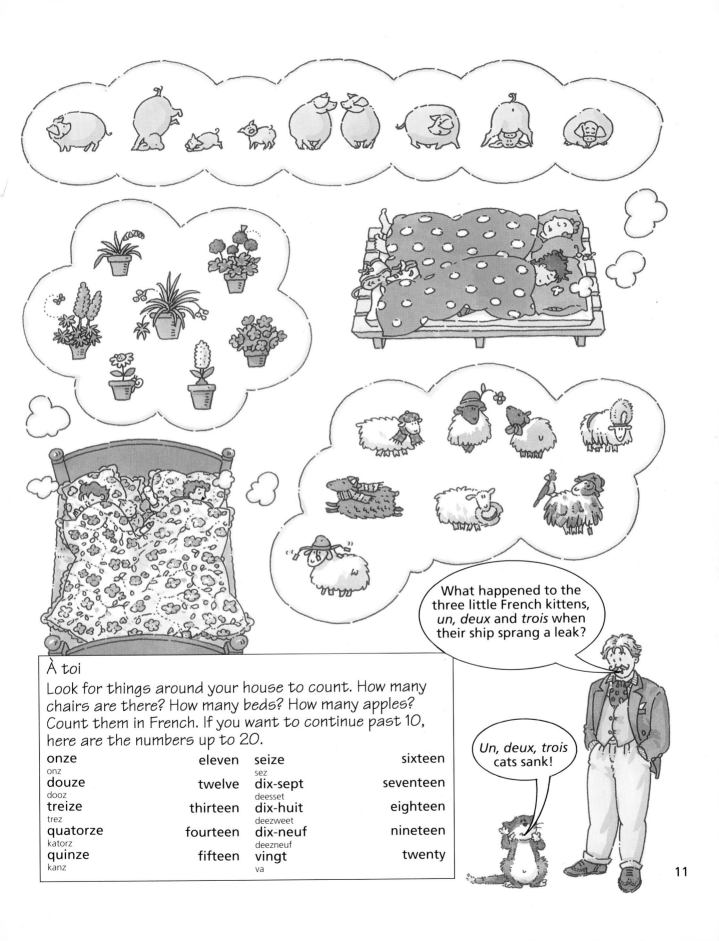

À toi

Look for things around your house to count. How many chairs are there? How many beds? How many apples? Count them in French. If you want to continue past 10, here are the numbers up to 20.

onze onz	eleven	seize sez	sixteen
douze dooz	twelve	dix-sept deesset	seventeen
treize trez	thirteen	dix-huit deezweet	eighteen
quatorze katorz	fourteen	dix-neuf deezneuf	nineteen
quinze kanz	fifteen	vingt va	twenty

What happened to the three little French kittens, *un, deux* and *trois* when their ship sprang a leak?

Un, deux, trois cats sank!

11

Jigsaw puzzles

The next morning everybody is tired and a little bit grumpy. Roger has brought down some jigsaw puzzles to try and cheer up the family. However, the pieces are all mixed up and Henri is the only one who can see what his puzzle is, *une pomme* (an apple).

Can you say in French what all the other puzzles should be? Use the picture list to help you. Only one of the missing pieces cannot be found anywhere. Who will not be able to finish their jigsaw?

Un and *une*

In French there are two ways to say "one", *un* or *une*. Both also mean "a" or "an". All *le* words are *un* words and all *la* words are *une* words.

Picture list

	une prune ewn prewn a plum		**un ananas** an ananass a pineapple		**une banane** ewn banan a banane		**une pêche** ewn pesh a peach
	une poire ewn pwar a pear		**une orange** ewn oronj an orange		**une pomme** ewn pom an apple		

À toi
See if you can remember the words for all these fruits and say what's in your fruit bowl at home.

12

Answer these questions out loud in French.

Can you see what Delphine is eating? What would Hercule like to eat?

Song

Here is a song about the fruit and vegetables that Delphine likes and dislikes. Can you guess what any of them are? You can see what all the words mean on page 32.

Au clair de la lu - ne, ma sou - ris Del - phine
oh clair de la lew nuh ma soo ree del feen

Aime beau - coup les pru - nes et les au - ber - gines.
em bo koo lay prew nuh ay laze oh bair jeen

Elle n'aime pas les oign - ons, ni les pet - its pois,
el nem pa laze on yaw nee lay pt ee pwa

Et pour tous les cham - pign - ons, elle les donne au roi.
ay poor too lay shom peen yaw el lay don oh rwa

13

Joke: What's blue and square? An orange in disguise

What is it?

Grand-mère has ordered lots of new things for her room. They have just been delivered. *Qu'est-ce que c'est?* [kess ke sai] means "what is it?"

Can you help the rest of the family say in French what is in each parcel? Say *c'est* [sai] which means "it is" and then the object. Use the picture list to help you with the names.

Remember that *un* and *une* both mean "a" as well as "one" in French.

Picture list

une table
ewn tabl
a table

une chaise
ewn shez
a chair

un lit
a lee
a bed

une télévision
tay lay veezee aw
television

un vase
a vaz
a vase

un réveil
a rave eye
an alarm clock

une lampe
ewn lomp
a lamp

une tasse
ewn tass
a cup

une assiette
ewn ass ee ett
a plate

À toi
Can you find all the things on the picture list in your own house? If you can, point to each one and say what it is in French, using *c'est* [sai] and then the name of the object.

Joke: What's this? It's this upside-down.

15

A day in the life of the Noisettes

This is a picture strip of a typical weekend day in the Noisette household - after a good night's sleep this time - but the pictures are all in the wrong order. Can you decide which order they should be in?

Use the word list to help you to say out loud what everyone is saying.

Word list

le petit déjeuner	breakfast
le ptee day je nay	
le déjeuner	lunch
le day je nay	
le dîner	dinner
le deenay	
du matin	in the morning
dew mata	
de l'après-midi	in the afternoon
de laprai meedee	
bonjour	hello, good morning
bonjoor	
bonsoir	good evening
bonswar	
bonne nuit	good night
bon nwee	
c'est	it is
sai	
dors bien	sleep well
dor beea	
il est 3 heures	it is three o'clock
eel ai trwazer	
il est 8 heures	it is eight o'clock
eel ai weeter	

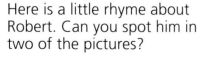

Here is a little rhyme about Robert. Can you spot him in two of the pictures?

> **Le petit lapin**
> le ptee lapa
> **Se lève le matin**
> se lev le mata
> **Puis venu le soir**
> pwee vin ew le swar
> **Il dit "au revoir".**
> eel dee orvwar

You can check what all the words mean on page 32.

16

Bon appétit [bon a ptee] is what you say before eating in France. It means "enjoy your meal".

À table [ah tabl] is how you tell people in French to come to the table.

Afternoon activity

This afternoon the Noisettes are all busy doing things in and around the house. Can you find someone doing each of the things on the word list somewhere in the big picture?

As you find each one, read out loud what that person is saying in French.

Word list

je mange	I am eating
je monj	
je lis	I am reading
je lee	
je cours	I am running
je koor	
je marche	I am walking
je marsh	
je chante	I am singing
je shont	
je bois	I am drinking
je bwa	
je parle	I am speaking
je parl	
je dors	I am sleeping
je dor	
je sors	I am going out
je sor	
je saute	I am jumping
je sote	
je travaille	I am working
je trav eye	
je tombe	I am falling
je tom b	
je nage	I am swimming
je naj	

À toi
Qu'est-ce que tu fais?
[kess ke tew fai]. What are you doing at the moment? You're probably reading, so you say *je lis* [je lee]. See if you can do all the other things in the picture and remember how to say them in French.

Joke: What has eight legs and spins? A spider in a washing machine.

19

Happy birthday

The next day is Grand-mère's birthday and the family is having a party for her. There are lots of different kinds of food because everyone likes different things.

To say you like something in French you say *j'aime* [jem] and then the thing you like. To say you don't like something you say *je n'aime pas* [je nem pa] and then the thing you don't like.

"Happy birthday" in French is *bon anniversaire* [bon anee vairsair].

J'aime le jambon.

Bon anniversaire.

J'aime le pain.

J'aime la confiture.

J'aime le chocolat.

Word list

j'aime	I like
jem	
je n'aime pas	I don't like
je nem pa	
moi	me
mwa	
les fruits	fruit
lay frwee	
le fromage	cheese
le fromaj	
le pain	bread
le pa	
les légumes	vegetables
lay laygewm	
la confiture	jam
la konfeetewr	
le chocolat	chocolate
le shokola	
la salade	salad
la sa lad	
le jambon	ham
le jombaw	
la soupe	soup
la soop	
les frites	french fries
lay freet	
les gâteaux	cakes
lay ga toe	
les saucisses	sausages
lay soseess	

Can you see which people do not like the food in front of them? Say out loud in French what they are thinking.

What do you think Sophie is saying? How would Hercule say what he likes in French?

À toi
Qu'est-ce que tu aimes manger? [kess ke tew em monjay] means "what *do* you like *to eat?*" Answer this question out loud in French. Remember, if you like something say *j'aime* [jem]. If you don't like something say *je n'aime pas* [je nem pa].

Le and *la* both change to *les* when you are talking about more than one thing.

21

Sophie goes shopping

Today is a school holiday and Sophie has gone to do the shopping.

Can you see from the picture what Sophie is asking for? *Je voudrais* [je voodray] means "I would like" and *et* [ay] means "and".

Now try to ask for all the items on Sophie's shopping list in French. Remember to say "please", *s'il vous plaît* [seel voo plai] and "thank you", *merci* [mairsee].

The money used in France is *francs* and *centimes*. There are 100 *centimes* to 1 *franc*.

Je voudrais un journal et une glace, s'il vous plaît.

Liste
4 pommes
9 bananes
8 petits pains
5 oignons
6 poissons
2 gâteaux

Can you see from the picture how to say "How much is it?" in French? Say it out loud.

What do you think Jean will ask for? Say it for him.

À toi
Combien [kombeea] means "how much" and "how many" in French. Can you answer the following questions by looking at the picture? Use the number reminder to help you count up in French how many there are.

Combien de fleurs?
Combien de chapeaux?
Combien de chats?

Number reminder

un	one	six	six
a		seess	
deux	two	sept	seven
deuh		set	
trois	three	huit	eight
trwa		weet	
quatre	four	neuf	nine
katr		neuf	
cinq	five	dix	ten
sank		deess	

Word list

je voudrais	I would like	**une fleur**	a flower
je voodray		ewn flur	
un chat	a cat	**un gâteau**	a cake
un sha		un ga toe	
une pomme	an apple	**une glace**	an ice cream cone
ewn pom		ewn glas	
une banane	a banana	**c'est combien?**	how much is it?
ewn banan		sai kombeea	
un petit pain	a roll	**c'est ... francs**	it is ... francs
un ptee pa		sai ... fraw	
un oignon	an onion	**s'il vous plaît**	please
un onyaw		seel voo plai	
un poisson	a fish	**merci**	thank you
un pwassaw		mairsee	
un journal	a newspaper	**un chapeau**	a hat
un joornal		un shapo	

Joke: What do you call a monkey who likes cakes? A meringue-utan.

23

Market day

Later on, the whole family goes down to the market. Everybody in the village seems to be there. It is so crowded that the Noisettes have split up and are all doing things in different parts of the market.

Jean asks where Robert is and the butcher points to him. *Où est* [oo ai] means "where is" and *Robert est là* [robair ai la] means "Robert is there".

Can you spot all of the Noisettes in the crowd? Point to each one and say that person's name followed by *est là* [ai la].

Où est Loulou?

Où est Delphine?

Où est Hercule?

Joke: Where are you going? I'm moving (house).

24

Dominoes to make

For something to do at home, Sophie and Henri have invented a game of dominoes which uses French colours. Here's how to make one like theirs and play it.

1. Cut your cardboard into 28 rectangles about 8cm long and 4cm wide (3in by 1½in). You can make the rectangles bigger if you have more cardboard.

4cm

8cm

You will need:
white cardboard (at least 32cm by 28 cm, 13in by 11in), felt tips, scissors and a black pen.

2. Copy the colours and words from the small dominoes shown here onto your rectangles. Use the colour guide to help you.

3. The idea of the game is to fit all the dominoes into a pattern, matching up the colours as shown below. If you are playing by yourself, the double-red starts.

rouge	rouge	rouge	rouge	rouge	rouge	rouge
rouge	bleu	vert	jaune	orange	violet	marron
bleu	bleu	bleu	bleu	bleu	bleu	orange
bleu	vert	jaune	orange	violet	marron	jaune
vert	vert	vert	vert	marron	orange	violet
vert	jaune	orange	violet	violet	marron	violet
jaune	jaune	jaune	jaune	orange	marron	marron
jaune	orange	marron	violet	orange	vert	marron

You can place doubles across the line, as shown here.

violet

violet

jaune

jaune

jaune

jaune

orange

ge

ouge

26

rouge

bleu

vert

vert

jaune

bleu

The domino line can turn corners.

rouge

rouge

bleu

marron

marron

vert

vert

vert
vair

marron
marraw

orange
oronj

violet
vee o lay

bleu
bleuh

jaune
jone

rouge
rooj

4. You can only add one domino to each colour and you must shout out the name of that colour before you put down your domino.

5. If you are playing with a friend, first spread the dominoes out, face-down, on the table or floor. Take seven dominoes each and put them face-up in front of you. These form your "hand".

6. The idea of this game is to get rid of all the dominoes in your hand and the first person to do so is the winner.

À toi

7. The first person to put down a double and shout out what colour it is (in French) starts. Take turns to match your dominoes with the colours or colour words at either end of the domino line, each time shouting out the colour in French before putting down your domino.

8. If you can't go, you must pick up a spare domino if there is one left, or miss a turn if there is not.

J'ai gagné.

| zéro | un | deux | trois | quatre | cinq | six |
| zayro | a | deuh | trwa | katr | sank | seess |

| zéro | deux | cinq | zéro | six | un | cinq |
| zayro | deuh | sank | zayro | seess | a | sank |

| trois | un | un | quatre | six | quatre | zéro |
| trwa | a | a | katr | seess | katr | zayro |

| quatre | trois | trois | six | deux | deux | cinq |
| katr | trwa | trwa | seess | deuh | deuh | sank |

Number dominoes

You could also make French number dominoes. Copy these dominoes onto pieces of cardboard (the same as the ones used for Colour dominoes) and play in the same way, this time matching up the number of objects with the number in French. The double-six fish starts.

27

Memory game

Here is a game which you can play again and again. The idea is to get to the finish as quickly as possible.

You will need:
a dice
a clock or watch

How to play

Look at the time when you start. Throw the dice and count with your finger the number of squares shown on the dice. Say the answer to the question on that square out loud then shake again.

If you land on a square with no question on it, shake again and move on.

All the answers can be found in this book, so if you can't remember or are not sure, look through the book until you find the correct answer.

Look at the time again when you finish. Can you do it more quickly next time?

How would you say the word for church in French, *l'église*?

1.lie gliss
2.lay gleez
3.liggles

Tell Henri how to ask for an ice cream cone in French.

Combien de fleurs?

Say "yes" in French.

Say "hi" in French.

What would Henri say if you asked, *Qu'est-ce que tu fais?*

Qu'est-ce que c'est?

How do you introduce yourself in French?

1.bleu
2.violet
3.jaune

Say "hello" in French.

Which of these describes Francine's balloon?

What is Sophie saying to Monsieur Vert?

Say "good night" in French.

Which of these is Sophie saying?

Say "I am eating" in French.

1.J'aime le fromage
2.J'aime le jambon
3.J'aime les bonbons

How will Henri tell his friend what Delphine's name is?

Départ
daypar
(start)

28

What comes after dix-huit?

Qu'est-ce que c'est?

Qu'est-ce que c'est?

How do you say "the garden" in French?

Which of these numbers is in the wrong place?

un
deux
cinq
trois
quatre

How would you ask for an apple in French?

How would you say "a peach" in French?

1. ewn peck
2. un pish
3. ewn pesh

Say the missing word, c'est une...

How do you say "my home" in French?

Qu'est-ce que c'est?

Say "thank you" in French.

20

How do you say "twenty" in French?

Which room do you think Hercule is in? Say it in French.

Qu'est-ce que c'est?

What happened to the three little French kittens, un, deux and trois, when their ship sprang a leak?

15

What comes after sept?

How do you say "fifteen" in French?

How will Sophie say what she is doing in French?

Qu'est-ce que c'est?

What do you say in France before starting a meal?

Qu'est-ce que c'est?

Say "good-bye" in French.

How do you say "how much is it?" in French?

Combien de pommes?

How would you say voici?

What would Jean say if you asked, Qu'est-ce que tu fais, Jean?

1. voy zee
2. vwasee
3. vwokay

Fin
fa
(end)

29

Word list

Here is a list, in alphabetical order, of all the French words and phrases used in this book. Use the list either to check quickly what a word means, or to test yourself. The [m] or [f] after *l'* words tell you whether the word is a *le* word (masculine) or a *la* word (feminine).

à pied	ah pee ay	*on foot*
à table	ah tabl	*dinner's ready!*
à toi	ah twa	*your turn*
ananas (l') [m]	ananass	*pineapple*
araignée (l') [f]	a renyay	*spider*
assiette (l') [f]	ass ee ett	*plate*
aubergine (l') [f]	oh bair jeen	*aubergine, eggplant*
au clair de	oh clair de	*by the light of*
la lune	la lewn	*the moon*
au revoir	orvwar	*goodbye*
banane (la)	banan	*banana*
beaucoup	bokoo	*a lot*
bleu	bleuh	*blue*
bon anniversaire	bon anee vairsair	*happy birthday*
bon appétit	bon a ptee	*enjoy your meal*
bonjour	bonjoor	*hello*
bonne nuit	bon nwee	*good night*
bonsoir	bonswar	*good evening*
ça use	sa ewz	*it wears out*
carré	karry	*square*
cave (la)	kaav	*cellar*
c'est	sai	*it is*
c'est combien?	sai kombeea	*how much is it?*
chaise (la)	shez	*chair*
chambre (la)	shombr	*bedroom*
champignon (le)	shompeenyaw	*mushroom*
chapeau (le)	shapo	*hat*
chat (le)	sha	*cat*
chez moi	shay mwa	*my home*
chocolat (le)	shokola	*chocolate*
cinq	sank	*five*
combien	kombeea	*how many, how much*
confiture (la)	konfeetewr	*jam*
cuisine (la)	kweezeen	*kitchen*
dans	daw	*in*
de l'après-midi	de laprai meedee	*in the afternoon*
déguisée	day geezay	*in disguise*
déjeuner (le)	day je nay	*lunch*
départ	daypar	*start*
deux	deuh	*two*
dîner (le)	deenay	*dinner*
dix	deess	*ten*

dix-huit	deezweet	*eighteen*
dix-neuf	deezneuf	*nineteen*
dix-sept	deesset	*seventeen*
dors bien	dor beea	*sleep well*
douze	dooz	*twelve*
du matin	dew mata	*in the morning*
école (l') [f]	aykol	*school*
église (l') [f]	aygleez	*church*
elle	el	*she, it*
elle est	el ai	*she is, it is*
elle est là	el ai la	*she/it is there*
elle s'appelle	el sapell	*she is called*
et	ay	*and*
ferme (la)	fairm	*farm*
fin	fa	*end*
fleur (la)	flur	*flower*
forêt (la)	foray	*forest*
frites (les) [f]	freet	*french fries*
fromage (le)	fromaj	*cheese*
fruit (le)	frwee	*fruit*
gâteau (le)	ga toe	*cake*
glace (la)	glas	*ice cream cone*
grand-mère (la)	gronmair	*grandmother*
grenier (le)	grin ee ay	*attic*
huit	weet	*eight*
il	eel	*he, it*
il dit	eel dee	*he says*
il est	eel ai	*he is, it is*
il est là	eel ai la	*he/it is there*
il s'appelle	eel sapell	*he is called*
il se lève	eel se lev	*he gets up*
j'ai gagné	jay ganyay	*I've won*
j'aime	jem	*I like*
jambon (le)	jombaw	*ham*
jardin (le)	jarda	*garden*
jardin public (le)	jarda pewbleek	*park*
jaune	jone	*yellow*
je	je	*I*
je bois	je bwa	*I am drinking*
je chante	je shont	*I am singing*
je cours	je koor	*I am running*
je déménage	je day may naj	*I am moving (house)*
je dors	je dor	*I am sleeping*
je lis	je lee	*I am reading*
je mange	je monj	*I am eating*
je m'appelle	je mapell	*I am called*
je marche	je marsh	*I am walking*

French	Pronunciation	English
je nage	je naj	I am swimming
je n'aime pas	je nem pa	I don't like
je parle	je parl	I am speaking
je saute	je sote	I am jumping
je sors	je sor	I am going out
je tombe	je tom b	I am falling
je travaille	je trav eye	I am working
je voudrais	je voodray	I would like
journal (le)	joornal	newspaper
kilomètre (le)	keelometr	kilometre
là	la	there
lampe (la)	lomp	lamp
lapin (le)	lapa	rabbit
le, la, les	le, la, lay	the
légume (le)	laygewm	vegetable
lit (le)	lee	bed
machine à laver (la)	masheen a lavay	washing machine
Madame	ma dam	Mrs.
magasin (le)	magaza	shop
maison (la)	mayzaw	house
maman	ma maw	mum
marron	marraw	brown
merci	mairsee	thank you
moi	mwa	me
Monsieur	missyer	Mr.
neuf	neuf	nine
non	naw	no
nous	noo	we, us
oignon (l') [m]	onyaw	onion
oncle (l') [m]	onkl	uncle
onze	onz	eleven
où est...?	oo ai	where is...?
où vas-tu?	oo va tew	where are you going?
oui	wee	yes
orange (l') [f]	oronj	orange
pain (le)	pa	bread
papa	papa	dad
patte (la)	pat	leg (of an animal)
pêche (la)	peach	peach
petit	ptee	small
petit déjeuner (le)	ptee day je nay	breakfast
petit pain (le)	ptee pa	roll
petits pois (les)	ptee pwa	peas
poire (la)	pwar	pear
poisson (le)	pwassaw	fish
pomme (la)	pom	apple

French	Pronunciation	English
pont (le)	paw	bridge
prune (la)	prewn	plum
puis	pwee	then
quatorze	katorz	fourteen
quatre	katr	four
qui	kee	who
quinze	kanz	fifteen
qu'est-ce que c'est?	kess ke sai	what is it?
qu'est-ce que tu aimes manger?	kess ke tew em monjay	what do you like to eat?
qu'est-ce que tu fais?	kess ke tew fai	what are you doing?
retourné	retoornay	upside-down
réveil (le)	rave eye	alarm clock
rivière (la)	reevee air	river
roi (le)	rwa	king
rouge	rooj	red
salade (la)	sa lad	salad
salle à manger (la)	sala monjay	dining room
salle de bain (la)	sal dba	bathroom
salon (le)	salaw	lounge
salut	salew	hello
saucisse (la)	soseess	sausage
seize	sez	sixteen
sept	set	seven
singe (le)	sanj	monkey
s'il vous plaît	seel voo plai	please
six	seess	six
soir (le)	swar	evening
souliers (les) [m]	soolee ay	shoes
soupe (la)	soop	soup
souris (la)	sooree	mouse
table (la)	tabl	table
tante (la)	tont	aunt
tasse (la)	tass	cup
télévision (la)	taylay veezee aw	television
tourne en rond	toorn aw raw	spins
treize	trez	thirteen
trois	trwa	three
tu	tew	you
un, une	a, ewn	a, one
vase (le)	vaz	vase
vert	vair	green
vingt	va	twenty
violet	vee o lay	purple
voici	vwasee	here is
zéro	zayro	zero

Answers

PAGE 4-5

Loulou passed *Oncle Paul, Monsieur Noisette, Robert, Tante Mirabelle, Jean, Roger, Sophie, Hercule, Francine, Henri, Grand-mère* and *Madame Noisette.*

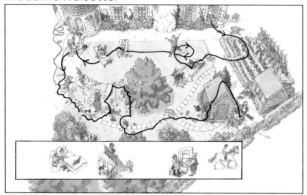

Sophie should say *Bonjour Loulou, Bonjour Henri* and *Bonjour Grand-mère.*

PAGE 6-7

This is the way you must go:

PAGE 10-11

Hercule fell asleep first - he only counted to five before falling asleep.

Try to learn the numbers in the number list. Then see if you can sing up to *dix kilomètres à pied* without looking at the number words.

The tune for the song is:

PAGE 12-13

What everyone's jigsaws were:
    Monsieur Noisette-*une pêche* (a peach),
    Tante Mirabelle-*une poire* (a pear),
    Suzanne-*une banane* (a banana),
    Francine-*un ananas* (a pineapple),
    Jean-*une prune* (a plum),
    Sophie-*une orange* (an orange).

Monsieur Noisette will not be able to finish his jigsaw.

The answers to the questions are:
    Delphine - *une prune* (a plum),
    Hercule - *une pomme* (an apple).

Here is what the words in the song mean in English:
    By the light of the moon
    My mouse Delphine
    Loves plums
    And aubergines.
    She doesn't like onions
    Nor peas
    And as for all the mushrooms
    She gives them to the king.

PAGE 16-17

The right order for the pictures is: D F G H B E C A

Here is the rhyme in English:
    My little rabbit
    Gets up in the morning
    And when evening comes
    He says "goodbye".

PAGE 20-21

Henri is thinking *Je n'aime pas le fromage.*
Roger is thinking *Je n'aime pas la soupe.*
Oncle Paul is thinking *Je n'aime pas les saucisses.*
Sophie is saying *J'aime les frites.*
Hercule would say *J'aime les fruits.*

PAGE 22-23

Sophie is asking for a newspaper and an ice cream cone.

"How much is it?" is *c'est combien?*

Jean is going to say *Je voudrais une glace, s'il vous plaît.*

There are:
    9 *fleurs*
    5 *chapeaux*
    6 *chats.*